John P. Coldstream

The Institutions of Italy

John P. Coldstream

The Institutions of Italy

ISBN/EAN: 9783337234928

Printed in Europe, USA, Canada, Australia, Japan

Cover: Foto ©Andreas Hilbeck / pixelio.de

More available books at **www.hansebooks.com**

THE INSTITUTIONS OF ITALY

THE
INSTITUTIONS
OF
ITALY

BY

JOHN P. COLDSTREAM
WRITER TO HER MAJESTY'S SIGNET
AUTHOR OF 'THE INSTITUTIONS OF AUSTRIA

𝔚estminster
ARCH. CONSTABLE AND CO.
Publishers to the India Office
2 WHITEHALL GARDENS, S.W.
MDCCCXCVI

Edinburgh : T. and A. CONSTABLE, Printers to Her Majesty

PREFACE

THE kind reception given to my book on the Institutions of Austria, published in July last, seems to justify the presentation of this volume to the public. It is not intended to be an exhaustive treatise on its subject, but is simply an endeavour to meet the felt want of a concise handbook giving such information on the Institutions of Italy as most travellers desire to have in passing through it, or as students wish to possess.

I could not have accomplished my object if I had not obtained the valued help of Signor Emilio Piovanelli, Professor of Letters of the University of Rome, and Clerk to the Chamber of Deputies for Telegraphic Reports, who supplied me with the information required, and to whom my best thanks are due. I have also to record my gratitude to Avvocato Adolfo de Bosis, Doctor of Laws of the University of Rome, for his kind help in the revision of the volume.

ROME,
1st *January* 1896.

CONTENTS

CHAPTER I

HISTORICAL AND GEOGRAPHICAL

CHAPTER II

GOVERNMENT

CHAPTER III

JUSTICE

The Courts of the Country—The Giudice Conciliatore—Its Jurisdiction—Its Judges—
The Pretura—Its Jurisdiction and Judges

CHAPTER IV

BETROTHAL AND MARRIAGE

CHAPTER V

SUCCESSION

CHAPTER VIII

RELIGION

·

CHAPTER IX

EDUCATION

CHAPTER X

THE LAND

CHAPTER XI

THE ARMY AND NAVY

CHAPTER XII

COMMERCE, TRADE, ETC.

CHAPTER XIII

THE RELIEF OF THE POOR

THE INSTITUTIONS OF ITALY

CHAPTER I

HISTORICAL AND GEOGRAPHICAL

IT is outside the scope of this work to give any detailed or adequate sketch of the history of Italy. Suffice it to say that since the fall of the Roman Empire there has never been a time when Italy could be called a united Kingdom till the present generation; that for many years before the time when it could be again spoken of as such, the country was divided into several States, chiefly ruled over by foreigners. Nation contended against nation for supremacy, while wars between the States themselves were not uncommon, and internal revolutions were the order of the day. At one time Austria, at another France, and even Spain ruled the country; while the Germans, to a certain extent, were not without their share of the spoil.

During the last hundred years, however, the spirit of independence and freedom arose among the people, and efforts were made to secure Italy for the Italians, and to have a free and united country. This, it may be said, after many years of valiant endeavour, amid much internal discord and bloodshed, and the interference—active and passive—of many of the Powers of Europe, she has now obtained, and at present she enjoys order, undisturbed either by internal discord or foreign intrigue.

In connection with the accomplishment of this unity, the names of Mazzini, King Charles Albert, Victor Emmanuel, Garibaldi, Manin, and Cavour stand prominently before the public, and should be honourably mentioned.

The work of unification was accomplished in 1870, since which time Italy has been, and still is, united as one Kingdom.

Before 1859 the country was divided into seven States, six of which, namely, Piedmont, Parma, Modena, Tuscany, the Papal States and Naples, were separate States with Kings or Dukes of their own as rulers, while the kingdom of Lombardy and Venice was subject to Austria.

In 1859 the kingdoms of Piedmont, Tuscany, Lombardy, Parma, and Modena were united in government; and in 1860 the northern parts of the Papal States, including Bologna, were added to the kingdom; while in 1861 Naples, in 1866 the Venetian provinces, and in 1870 Rome and the rest of the Papal States, became part of the Kingdom.

Turin had been the capital and seat of government of Piedmont, but in 1865 Florence was recognised as the capital and seat of government in the new Kingdom, and existed as such till 1870, when the seat of government was transferred to Rome on the evacuation of the French and Papal troops.

The unification of Italy has been productive of the greatest good to its people. Education has made great progress, as will be gathered from the sequel. The material wealth of the country increases rapidly notwithstanding the heavy taxation imposed. This, however, is not in excess, but very much under that of France per head of population. Commendatore Cerboni, an authority upon the subject, has stated that whereas Italy was taxed at about 45 francs 24 cents per head of population, in France the amount was 84 francs 44 cents.

The sanitary condition and general health of the community has greatly improved under the changed state of affairs and government.

The people feel that they are now living under free institutions, and that they themselves are the rulers of their own destinies so far as it can lie with them to be so.

Italy is a peninsula, and is bounded on the north by France, Switzerland, and Austria, while its eastern border is bounded by the Adriatic Sea, and the south and west by the Mediterranean. It has 69 provinces, and the following are its divisions, viz.:—Piedmont, Lombardy, Venetia, Liguria, Emilia, Tuscany, Marche, Abruzzi, Lazio, Campania, Puglie, Basilicata, Calabria, Sicily, and Sardinia.

The capital of the Kingdom is Rome, while Naples is the most populous of its cities; the other chief cities are Milan, Florence, Venice, and Turin.

The chief rivers are the Po, the Adige, the Tiber, and the Arno.

The chief mountains in the Alpine range are Mont Blanc, Monte Rosa, and Grand Paradiso. In the Appenines, the chief is the Gran Sasso d'Italia. In Sicily there is Mount Etna, which, with Vesuvius near Naples, are the only two great volcanoes in Europe.

The chief lakes are Maggiore, Como, Lugano, and Garda.

The population of the Kingdom is 31,250,000, of whom 135,000 are French, and reside chiefly in Piedmont; 55,000 are Albanians; 20,000 are Greeks, chiefly found in Calabria and Sicily; 20,000 are Germans, chiefly to be found near Verona; 5500 are English, scattered through the country.

A census is usually taken every ten years; but to save the expense, the last, which should have been taken in 1891, was not taken up. The figures given above are for 1895, and are taken from the Registrar's returns, which are kept with amazing accuracy.

The superficial area of the Kingdom is about 73,221,413 acres, and the proportion of population to the square mile is about 272, while that of the United Kingdom of Great Britain and Ireland is 338; Germany, 236; France, 184; Austria-Hungary, 171; Spain, 91; and Russia, 47.

CHAPTER II

GOVERNMENT

THE Government of Italy is a Monarchy, limited and controlled by Parliament. The Monarch bears the title of 'By the Grace of God and will of the Nation, King of Italy.' He chooses his own Ministers of State, and with their advice he can declare war, and make peace; he can pardon criminals, and reduce sentences; he can put his veto on any measures passed by Parliament, and he can dissolve Parliament.

The present King is Humbert I. He was born on 14th March 1844, was married to Margherita, Princess of Savoy, daughter of the Duke of Genoa, in April 1868, and he succeeded his father, Victor Emmanuel, on 9th January 1878.

The successor to the throne is Victor Emmanuel, Prince of Naples, the only child of King Humbert. He was born on 11th November 1869, and is still unmarried.

The King has a personal allowance of 14,250,000 lire,[1] paid out of the taxes of the country.

THE PARLIAMENT.

The Parliament is the only Legislative Assembly in the kingdom. It is the same in constitution, and follows the model of Piedmont, founded in 1848.

---

[1] A lira is equal to a franc, or about 10d. stg.

It consists of two Chambers—an Upper and a Lower House. The Upper House is called 'The Senate,' while the Lower is styled 'The House of Deputies.'

THE SENATE.

There is no limit to the number of the members of the Senate. At present it consists of about 300 Senators.

The ordinary members of the Senate are, on the advice of his Ministers, nominated by the King for life. Their appointment must, however, be ratified by the Senate itself; and in two cases at least, during the last few years, such ratification has been refused. There are no hereditary members except Princes of the Royal Family, who become Senators on attaining the age of twenty-one.

The other members are chosen from out of twenty-one classes of the community; but practically they may be said to be selected from the following, viz. :—

(1) Men who have distinguished themselves by service to the State.

(2) Men who have been elected members of the House of Deputies for three Parliaments.

(3) Men who pay over 3000 lire of taxes yearly.

(4) Men distinguished in science, art, and literature, professional men, etc., etc.

There is no particular time for appointing new members to the Senate. As Senators die their places may, or may not, be at once filled up; and it often happens that new members are appointed simply for the purpose of preventing a Government measure from being lost, or as the exigencies of the Government of the day require it.

The members of the Senate receive no remuneration for their services, but they have free passes on the railways and on the steamboats whenever they travel.

There are a President, and four Vice-Presidents, who must be members of the House. They are nominated by the King. They have no salaries.

The Ministers or Secretaries of State are twelve in number, and can be members of either the Senate or of the House of Deputies. They have salaries of about £1000 each. They are appointed by the King, and they hold Portfolios as follows, viz. :—

(1) The President of the Council, who

may also fill a Secretaryship; (2) Home Affairs, called the Minister of the Interior; (3) Foreign Affairs; (4) War; (5) Navy; (6) Public Instruction; (7) Trade, Commerce, and Agriculture; (8) Public Works; (9) Post and Telegraphs; (10) Justice and Religion ; (11) Finance; (12) The Treasury.

There is an Under-Secretary attached to the office of each Secretary of State, who must be a member of one or other of the Houses, and can represent his chief in it.   Their salaries are £400 each.

The Ministers can introduce measures in either House, and can speak in both.

For the transaction of business the Senate is divided into five Committees.

When a bill is introduced by a Minister it is read a first time in the House, and then sent to be considered by all these

Committees, each of which discusses it, and appoints one of their number to form another Committee of five (one being taken from each Committee) to report upon it to the Senate. The report of this latter Committee may be that of a majority of its members. When presented to the House it is supported by one or more of its members, and should it not be a unanimous report, the minority is also represented. It is then discussed by the members of the House at large, and if the bill is to proceed, the clauses of it are gone over and adjusted, when it is read over a third time and voted on. The voting takes place by the members depositing in black and white vases balls of like colours. If they approve of a measure they place a white ball in the white vase,

and also a black ball in the black vase.
If they disapprove, they place a black ball
in the white vase, and a white ball in the
black one.

If the bill introduced is that of a private
member, before it is allowed to be read
even a first time it must be sent to the
five Committees; and if they approve of
its principle, it is again presented to the
House, and is then treated in the same
manner as if it were a Government Bill.

Any measure except a Finance Bill can
be considered by the Senate in the first
instance.

A bill dealing with Finance must be
brought in in the Lower House.

The Senate can meet at any time when
summoned by the King. Its usual Sessions
are held between 15th November and

15th July, with two intervals of twenty days each, or more, at Christmas and at Easter.

HOUSE OF DEPUTIES.

The House of Deputies is the Lower House of Parliament, and its members are elected by the people.

It consists of 508 members, whose only qualification, except as regards officers in the army and navy, is that they must be Italian subjects, and not less than thirty years of age. Among the members may be found judges, professors, professional men, clergymen, noblemen, etc., etc.; but of men holding office under Government, exclusive of the Ministers of State, not more than forty can be members of the House, and of these forty, not more than ten

can be Professors in the Universities. The
officers of the army and navy who can be
members of the House must in the army
hold at least the rank of Major, and in
the navy that of Captain. The working
classes are not represented to any great
extent by men of their own position; but
in the present Parliament the Chief Fac-
chino, or Head Porter of Milan, represents
one of the districts of that city.

The members receive no salary, but
have, like members of the Senate, free
passes on all the railways, and on the
steamboats. In the latter they can travel
as far as Constantinople.

A member on his election receives a
gold medal, about the size of an English
sovereign, which he usually attaches to
his watch-chain, and this is his pass in

travelling. Many members have several of these medals attached to their chains, indicating of how many Parliaments they have been members.

The Parliament is elected for five years, but it may be dissolved by the King at any time on the advice of his Ministers. The average duration of a Parliament since its creation has been about two and a half years. The shortest was about five months, and the longest four and a half years.

The electors are all male subjects of Italy of twenty-one years of age and upwards, who are able to read and write, and who must prove it if called on to do so; besides (1) have the licence of the Elementary Schools; or (2) be in such a position as justifies this presumption; or

(3) pay 19 lire—18 centimes of direct taxation annually; or (4) what is deemed equivalent to the last, as paying 500 lire rental for land; or for a house, from 150 lire in rural Communes, increasing in ratio to 400 lire in the largest Communes.

A register of voters is made up by every municipality, who are supposed to know about every qualified voter within their bounds. No fixed period of residence within the voting district is required, and if a voter changes his residence, on notice given, he can have his name transferred to the register of his new abode; but if he does not take such steps, his name will remain on the register of his former abode till so transferred; but this can be done only once a year.

The Kingdom is divided into equal

electoral districts, of as nearly 50,000 electors as possible, each of which returns one member. There are 5 members for Rome, 12 for Naples, and 6 for Milan. The voting is by ballot, but the elector must write out on his voting-card the name of the candidate for whom he votes.

Should no candidate have an actual majority of votes in a district a second ballot takes place, on the lapse of a week from the first. If one-eighth of the voters has not voted, another election is held within eight days.

The elections always take place on a Sunday, so as to give an opportunity to the small shopkeepers and labourers, who otherwise would have difficulty in voting, to exercise their right of franchise.

The official expenses of the election are borne by the Commune.

The personal expenses of the candidate, and of his candidature, are borne by himself or by any society or organisation which brings him forward. There is no limit to the amount of these expenses, which may only be a few pounds, but have been quoted as high as £4000.

Bribery at elections is forbidden by law, but it constantly takes place. There is a special Committee of Parliament to inquire into cases of this kind, which is nominated by the President. On proof of bribery being established the election is declared null, and a new one takes place.

The President of the House is elected by its members for one Session only. There are four Vice-Presidents elected in like manner. Neither the President nor the Vice-Presidents have any salary.

The President sits in the centre of a long platform, having the officials of Parliament sitting at desks on either side of him. Neither he nor they have any robes of office. He calls the House to order by the ringing of a small handbell, which does not appear always to be effective.

The Ministers sit before a long table, below the President's platform and facing the members, who are seated opposite on benches rising from the floor of the House in a semicircle. Each member has his own particular seat with a desk on which he can place his papers. This he occupies during the whole of the Parliament for which he is elected. A plan of the House can be obtained on which is indicated the seat of each member, so that, as a rule, it can be at once ascertained by reference to it who is addressing the House.

On the' left of the President sits a gentleman holding the office styled 'Rivisore dei resoconti parlamentari,' whose duty is to send, as the proceedings go on, a *résumé* of them to all the Prefects in the various provinces by telegram. There sit in the middle of the floor of the House, at a separate table, three of the fifteen short-hand reporters appointed by the Parliament, who make up the official report of the proceedings of which each member receives a copy. The Ministers, and other members, if they desire it, are, before publication, given an opportunity of revising their speeches for this report.

Facing the table of the Ministers sit the

Committee of nine appointed to bring up the report of the bill under discussion.

At the commencement of each new Parliament the members are sworn in a body; the President saying, 'I swear to be faithful to the King, and to be faithful to all the laws of the State for the good of the King and country'; while the members one by one say, 'I swear.'[1]

Bills are introduced and dealt with in the same manner as those in the Senate (see page 14), except that the number of Committees which consider them is nine in place of five. Besides which there is a permanent Committee for Finance.

The quorum of the House required for the passing of a measure, or of a bill, is

[1] The same oath is taken by the Senators on their nomination only.

the half of its members, exclusive of those who have obtained leave of absence. Voting takes place on bills in the same way as that already described in the Senate (see page 15); but when a resolution is proposed, the voting may take place by the names of the members being called over, when they indicate their opinion by answering, Yes, or No. In the House of Deputies this operation occupies about an hour.

Interrogations are, at the opening of each sederunt, addressed to the Ministers. These are printed in the orders of the day. It is the rule of the House that only forty minutes should be allowed for this purpose; but it often happens that more time is occupied if a discussion arises. In this others than the questioner and Minister are allowed to take part. Questions not answered within the time allotted are postponed to, and taken up, the following day.

After questions are finished for the day, the House applies itself, chiefly on Mondays, to the interpellations. These are not properly questions, but refer to matters of public interest or Government policy, and the interpellante can close his speech with a resolution. He is allowed to speak at length, as is also the Minister who replies.

Except in speaking to an interrogation, when, by the rules of the House, a member is limited to five minutes, no limit is put upon the speeches of members.

There are three leading political parties in Parliament, named as follows, viz.:—
(1) 'The Right,' or the Conservative Party,

who at present constitute about one-quarter of the House, and sit on the right of the President; (2) 'The Left,' or the Liberal Party, who sit on the left of the President; and (3) 'The Centre,' or Independent Party, who sometimes vote with the Right, and sometimes with the Left.

The Left and the Centre constitute together, at present, three-quarters of the House.

The Liberal Party is divided, at the present moment, into four factions, viz. :— (1) the Socialists, of whom there are 6; (2) the Radicals, of whom there are 50; (3) the Advanced Liberals, of whom there are about 100; and (4) the Liberals proper. For practical purposes, however, the House resolves itself into the two divisions of the Ministerialists and the Opposition.

The House meets at 2 P.M., and rises usually at 6.30; but when business requires it sits as late as 10 o'clock. During the Session (see page 16) it sits every day in the week except Sunday, and even on Sundays, if necessary, while morning sittings at 10 o'clock are sometimes held.

Admission to the House is obtained by order from the President, or from a member. The general public are admitted to various Tribunes at the back of the members' seats, some of which are reserved for ladies, who are not screened from the public gaze. In the gallery, at the back of the President's chair, are Tribunes specially reserved for the Royal party, Ex-Deputies, and the President's and

Ministers' friends; while to the right is a large Tribune for the Ambassadors and their friends.

The House of Deputies is the Palazzo di Monte-Citorio, close to the Piazza Colonna, Rome. It was not specially built for its present purpose, but was, before 1870, the place of meeting of the Courts of Justice. The Senate meets in a separate building, the Palazzo Madama, built by Catherine de Medici.

When a Minister of State or a Senator requires to be prosecuted for his official acts, he is tried before the Senate, sitting as a Court of Justice.

The taxes imposed by Parliament are:—
(1) Income Tax, which is assessed, not according to the amount of a man's income, but according to its nature and source. At

present it varies from $7\frac{1}{2}$ to 20 per cent.[1]
(2) Property and Land Tax; (3) Death
duties, both on heritable and moveable
property, which are taxed equally; (4)
Customs duties, which are imposed on
nearly all imports, but such as are charged
on the raw material can be recovered when
it is manufactured.

The highest taxation imposed is that on
land, which is taxed at 30 per cent., and
in some cases even 40 and 50 per cent., but
this is taken into account in the purchas-
ing of land, which is generally bought to

---

[1] The following are the grades of the Income Tax
at present, viz. :—

A.—On interest of Rentes,	.	20 per cent.
,, Mortgages,	.	15 ,,
B.—On profits of Industries,		10 ,,
C.—On Professional Incomes,		9 ,,
D.—On Clerks' Salaries,	.	$7\frac{1}{2}$,,

yield, after paying all taxes and burdens, about 3 per cent., although it may sometimes be acquired to yield even higher rates.

Including all taxes and rates, a man with an average income will pay from 10 to 15 per cent. of taxation in all; but even from 40 to 50 per cent. is paid by some persons.

The total revenue for the Kingdom for 1894-95 was 1,699,236,025 lire, or about £67,969,441 sterling; while the expenditure was 1,695,499,764 lire, or about £67,819,990. The national debt is about 10,000,000,000 lire, or £400,000,000, on which there is an annual charge of 463,351,362 lire, or £14,534,014.

THE CONSIGLIO PROVINCIALE.

This is the Assembly of the various Provinces of Italy. It has administrative functions only.

There are 69 such Councils in the Kingdom. Their duties are to attend to the roads, the hospitals and charities, the secondary education of the Province, and to administer its property.

The number of the members of a Council depends upon the population of the Province. If there is a population of 600,000, there will be sixty members of the Council. If the population is under 20,000, the Council will consist of twenty members.

The President of the Council must be

a member of it, and is elected by the votes of his colleagues for one session only.

The members of the Council must be twenty-one years of age, and pay a certain amount of taxation, and also be able to read and write. They are not paid for their services.

They are elected for six years, but one-half of the Council retires every three years, when new elections take place. There is no second ballot in a provincial election.

The electors must be twenty-one years of age, be able to read and write, and pay a certain amount of taxation. They vote only for those who are to represent the particular district in which they are qualified as voters.

The Council bears all the official expenses of the election.

The sole source of the revenue of the Council is the taxation they impose on land.

The representative of the Government in the Province is the Prefect, who resides in its chief city. He is represented by a Vice-Prefect in the smaller cities. He is Chief of the Police, but has no judicial functions. He is named by the Government, and holds office during their pleasure. He may be transferred from one Province to another. The Prefects are of three classes : those of the first class receive 12,000 lire of salary; those of the second class 10,000; those of the third class 9000; in addition to which they receive an allowance for expenses varying from 3000 to 20,000 lire a year, according to the size and importance of the Provinces to which they are appointed.

THE CONSIGLIO COMUNALE.

This Assembly is the Council of the Commune, and is only administrative in its character.

A Commune is not a mere parish. It may be only one parish, or a combination of parishes, or a town of greater or less extent. It may be added to or taken from, but that only by Act of Parliament. The Consiglio Comunale is somewhat equivalent to the Parish and Town Councils of Great Britain.

There are about 8250 such Councils in Italy. The duty of the Council is to attend to elementary education, the making and repairing of roads and streets, the drainage of the town or district, as also registration of births, marriages, and deaths, and the keeping of the register of electors of Parliament.

As a rule, private companies supply the Communes with gas and water in Italy.

The number of members of a Consiglio Comunale is eighty where the population of the Commune is over 250,000, and fifteen where it is under 3000.

The qualification of members and electors is the same as that for the Consiglio Provinciale.

The electors vote, however, only for four-fifths of the members to be elected—thus, if eighty members are to be elected, each elector can vote for sixty-four; and in this way, to some extent, minorities can be represented.

The members are elected for six years, but one-half of them retire every third year.

The elections take place on Sunday.

There is no second ballot, as for a Parliamentary Election.

The official expenses of the election are borne by the Council.

The President of the Consiglio Comunale is called the Syndic. He is elected for three years, and that by the Council in all Communes, except for such as have only a population of less than 10,000, not being the capital of a Province, when he is nominated by the King.

The Syndic has no salary, but in large cities he has an allowance for expenses, as for example in Rome, where he has about £500 a year.

He is the administrator of the Commune, and where there is no Prefect he is also the representative of the Government.

He may be of any occupation, and in rural districts he frequently is a peasant.

The Revenue of the Commune is raised from taxes on carriages, horses, servants, a tax known as the 'family tax'—imposed rather in an arbitrary manner in accordance with the style in which a man lives—and the local Octroi, known as 'Dazio Consumo,' or petty customs upon articles coming into the Communes for consumption, which are levied at the gates or entrance to the cities.

CHAPTER III

JUSTICE

THE Courts of Justice of Italy are as follows:—

1. The Giudice Conciliatore.
2. The Pretura, or Court of the Pretore.
3. The Tribunal.
4. The Court of Assise.
5. The Court of Appeal.
6. The Court of Cassation.

THE GIUDICE CONCILIATORE.

This Court is one in which petty cases, chiefly those of small debts up to one hundred lire in amount, are brought.

There is no appeal from this Court except on the ground of incompetency, and that to the Tribunal. The judges of this Court need not be trained lawyers. They hold their appointment for three years only, and have no salary. The parties, or others on their behalf—not necessarily an avvocato —can plead in person in this Court.

In large cities there is generally one Court of this kind for about every 50,000 inhabitants, but it varies according to the amount and importance of the business.

THE PRETURA.

This is a Court of first instance, and is the Court of the Pretore, where causes not exceeding in value 1500 lire can be brought. Its criminal jurisdiction extends to cases: (1) where the limit of punishment is three months' imprisonment; or (2) without actual imprisonment, one year's confinement within the bounds of a Commune; or (3) a fine not exceeding 2000 lire.

There is an appeal to the Court of the Tribunal, both in civil and criminal cases; but in the latter, not on the facts or guilt, but solely on procedure and points of law.

One judge only—the Pretore—presides in this Court. His salary is 2500 lire per annum. When appointed, he is generally a young man of about twenty-five years, and he may remain in this Court all his life.

There are about 1500 Courts of the Pretore in the Kingdom. There is generally one for every 50,000 inhabitants.

THE TRIBUNAL.

This Court is also one of first instance as well as of appeal from the Pretore.

Its jurisdiction extends to cases of all kinds and amounts, limited as *infra*. It has power to call in the assistance of two Merchant Assessors, in commercial cases, but in practice it seldom or ever does so.

Three judges, including the President, sit in this Court. The President has a salary of from 5000 to 7000 lire, while the other judges receive from 3500 to 4500 lire.

Such criminal cases as do not involve more than one year's imprisonment can be tried in this Court, and that without a jury —a jury in this Court not being allowed. A case of murder cannot be tried here.

There is an appeal from a decision from the Tribunal to the Court of Appeal.

There is a Tribunal in every large city and town in Italy, and there are 162 Courts of this kind in the Kingdom.

THE COURT OF APPEAL.

This Court is one solely for appeals from the Tribunal. There are twenty such Courts in Italy. Five judges sit in it. They have salaries of 6000 lire, except the President, whose salary is 7000 lire.

THE COURT OF ASSISE.

This is a Court for criminal cases only. Its jurisdiction extends to all cases of crime which are not specially appropriated to the cognisance of the other Courts.

Three judges sit in this Court. The President has a salary of 7000 lire, while the others receive 6000 lire each.

Criminal cases can be tried by a jury in this Court. Thirty persons qualified to be jurors are summoned for each case, to eight of whom the Prosecutor can object, and the accused person can also object to a like number. Fourteen being thus left, twelve are empanelled to try the case, and two remain in attendance in Court to take the place of any juryman who may be taken ill, or otherwise fails.

The verdict may be given by a majority, but if the jury are equally divided in opinion the accused is acquitted.

A person qualified to be a juror must be over thirty and under sixty-five years of age. He must be able to read and write, and be in that position of life which fits him for the office. Persons who hold high office, or who have the cure of souls, or whose place in office or business cannot be supplied, are exempt from serving as jurymen. Jurors are only paid their expenses.

From the Court of Assise there is an appeal upon procedure and questions of law, but not upon the facts of the case or the guilt of the accused, to the Court of Cassation, and that within one month.

THE COURT OF CASSATION.

This is the highest Court of Appeal in the Kingdom. It has both a civil and a criminal jurisdiction.

There are five such Tribunals or divisions of this Court, which sit in various cities of the Kingdom; but at present there is a tendency to concentrate their business in Rome, and, as a matter of fact, so as to secure uniformity of judgment, all criminal, and nearly all civil, cases coming before this Court are now tried in Rome.

The full sederunt of the Cassation is one of seven judges.

The first President of the Court has a salary of 15,000 lire, or £600; while the second President receives 12,000 lire, and the other judges 9000 lire each.

In a criminal case the judges do not give judgment, in the proper sense of the term, after hearing it, but they indicate their opinion upon it, and remit it to another Court of Assise or Appeal from that from which it came, that it may be tried again if necessary, and judgment be pronounced.

In a civil case, on the other hand, the Court of Cassation, after hearing the case, gives judgment in common form.

PROCEDURE.

(a) *Civil,*

Briefly, the course of procedure in a civil cause is as follows :—

In an ordinary case the plaintiff, called 'attore,' obtains a citation from the officers of the Court, with which the defendant (convenuto) is served, and thereafter he is again served with a short notice of claim, called 'comparsa,' to which an answer (risposta) is given, which the plaintiff can answer by another document, called 'replica,' and the defendant can then lodge a further plea in answer, called 'contra-replica.'

The parties require to appear before the judge by their avvocato within from ten to twenty-five days, or even longer, after the first citation, according to the distance of their place of jurisdiction from the Court, the cause being then in the rolls of the Court for the first time. At this diet it is usual to ask for a short adjournment. When the case is next called, the avvocato for each party appears with his brief or statement, and pleads his case before the judges. At the close of the argument the brief of the avvocato for each party is handed to the judges, who consider them in chambers, and thereafter give judgment. If a proof of the statements of the parties is required, it is taken either by commission, or by a member of the Court.

D

There is no trial by jury in civil cases in Italy.

There is no record of the case made up in the form of statement and answer, and, except in the case of appeal, the printing of the pleadings is not, as a rule, resorted to.

The time for taking an appeal from the Court of the Pretura is thirty days, and from that of the Tribunal sixty days.

When a person desires to bring an action of damages for injury against another, he presents a querela (demand for prosecution) to the Questura Office (Police Office), and thereafter his avvocato has, in the first place, to submit the facts of the case to a Committee of the Tribunal specially appointed to deal with the cause at this stage. The judges hear the avvocato upon it, and, if a *prima facie* case is made out, leave is granted to bring the case into Court.

The conduct of the case, up to the lodging of the last written pleading, is undertaken by the procuratore (solicitor). Thereafter the cause is in the hands of the avvocatos of the parties without the intervention of a solicitor.

At the present time the course of litigation is long and tedious, but efforts are being made to shorten and simplify it.

(b) *Criminal.*

In serious criminal cases, the public prosecutor — Procuratore del Re — must bring the action. He goes to the spot and inquires into the circumstances of the crime. Immediately after arrest the accused is examined. If the penalty for the crime is under three years' imprisonment, he can be released on bail, and if it be under three months, he is freed from custody at once to await his trial. Thereafter there is a preliminary inquiry by the Giudici Istruttore, who determines if there is a *prima facie* case. If there is, the accused is cited for the appropriate Court. There is, however, no fixed time within which an accused person must be cited for trial, and often he remains in prison for an unduly long period of time before being tried.

At the trial the President states the case to the jury. The examination of the accused then takes place. The witnesses are then examined, and thereafter the accused is asked if he has anything to add. The accused and the witnesses are examined by the judge himself. The prosecutor and the counsel for the accused can also examine them, but all the questions must be put through the President of the Court.

After evidence is led the public prosecutor and the accused's counsel address the jury, the public prosecutor can reply, and then the counsel for the prisoner is always entitled to the last word. The judge then sums up the evidence, and the jury retire to consider their verdict, which may be given by a majority, but if the jury are equally divided in opinion the accused is acquitted.

After the verdict is given the public prosecutor asks that the penalty appropriate to the particular crime should be inflicted. There is a code of punishment prescribing a certain minimum and a certain maximum penalty for crimes, but the proper punishment within these limits is left to the discretion of the judge.

The witnesses are sworn, and take the oath in these terms: 'I swear to tell the truth, the whole truth, and nothing but the truth.'

The jurors are not sworn as a body, but in presenting their verdict their chairman says: 'On my honour and on my conscience, the verdict of the jury is this,' etc.

For murder, capital punishment does not exist—the appropriate punishment being imprisonment for life.

Imprisonment for debt, once competent, is now abolished.

There is no recognised official report of cases, civil or criminal, but there are private reports of such which are allowed to be referred to in Court.

THE JUDGES.

The judges of Italy are not, as a rule, appointed from among the members of the practising bar, although occasionally an avvocato (but of not less than six years' standing), who finds he has not the necessary forensic power to succeed as a pleader, applies for and obtains the appointment of a judge.

At the beginning of his career, as a rule, a lawyer must choose the judicial branch of his profession if he desire office as a judge. To qualify as such he must take the degree of Doctor of Laws at a University, and also pass the special Judge Examination. It is also necessary for him to attend in the offices of the Court for some time. For his first appointment he receives a judgeship in the Court of the Pretura, as a rule. From this Court he may be, and generally is, by merit and seniority, promoted from one Court to another, till he receives the appointment of a judge of the Court of Cassation, which he generally does about the age of fifty-five. There he can remain till unfit for duty. He can then retire on a pension equal to about two-thirds of his salary.

The political proclivities of a man are, it is said, in no case taken into account either in his first appointment or his subsequent promotion, but there is no doubt it is of advantage to him if he has friends among the ministers.

The judges wear black robes with stiff round hats in Court on ordinary occasions, but those of the highest degree on important occasions wear scarlet robes faced with ermine.

Of judges of all classes it is computed that there are about 4500 or 5000 in Italy.

THE AVVOCATO.

The avvocato is not admitted to practice in Italy till he is twenty-five years of age. He must possess the degree of Doctor of Laws from some University in Italy; he must also pass the Bar Examination, chiefly dealing with the practice of the Court. He must likewise have been in attendance in the chambers of a practising avvocato for some years. He is admitted to practice at the bar by an Act of Court. An avvocato may make an income from his fees of from £300 to £1600 a year, and in Genoa and Naples, it is said, some avvocatos make as much as £4000 per annum.

Some avvocatos are also qualified as solicitors and when this is the case they can undertake the whole management of a case from its beginning to its close. The fees payable by an avvocato on admission to practice are only about 100 lire (£4), and that to the Society of Avvocatos to which he may belong.

THE SOLICITOR.

The solicitor, styled procuratore, must take the degree of Doctor of Laws. Thereafter he requires to attend for one year at least in the chambers of a solicitor, and when about the age of twenty-five he is admitted to practice by an Act of Court. The fees payable to his Corporation are only about £4. The duty of a solicitor chiefly consists in preparing the pleadings in cases, up to the time when the avvocato takes charge of the case, but he is also permitted to plead in the Court of the Conciliatore, and Pretura.

THE NOTARY.

The notaro requires only to study law in the University for two years. He need not take a degree in Law. He has to attend for two years in the chambers of a notary, and when about twenty-five years of age he is admitted to practice by an

Act of the Court. His duty is to attend to the preparation of wills, conveyances of property, contracts, and all documents requiring legal knowledge and accuracy for their preparation. It is not the custom in Italy for a notary to act as executor or trustee under wills, although he occasionally does so, but he frequently acts as liquidator of companies or estates.

THE POLICE.

There are in Italy three distinct classes of police, viz. :—(1) The Carabinieri, who are the military or War Office police, but they also act under the orders of the Home Office. They are chiefly to be found in the Campagna or country districts, and are employed both in civil and criminal matters and investigations.

(2) The Guardie di Pubblica Sicurezza, are the police for criminal affairs in towns. They are appointed by the Home Office, but they are under the orders of the prefect. (3) The Guardie Municipale are the special officers of the municipality in towns. They attend to the carrying out of the orders of the Syndic and Municipal authorities, as to the public safety and sanitary condition, but they are not criminal officers proper. They are appointed by the Syndic.

CHAPTER IV

BETROTHAL AND MARRIAGE

In Italy, except it be among some noble houses where the preservation of family estates enters into consideration, the young people are, as a rule, allowed to exercise their own choice in the selection of their partners in life.

Marriage takes place, in many cases, at a very early age, and bridegrooms and brides of seventeen and sixteen years of age, even among the best families, are not unknown.

There is no formal betrothal as a custom, nor any intimation of the engagement by cards sent to friends by parents of the engaged couple, as is common in some other European countries.[1]

The following persons cannot inter-marry. A man cannot marry his deceased wife's sister, nor a woman her deceased husband's brother.

[1] In Storey's *Roba di Roma*, p. 496, he says: 'Among the families of wealth and rank at Rome the capitoli or betrothal' (but the word capitoli signifies the signing of the contract rather than the time of betrothal) 'is a much more important and festal ceremony than that of marriage. Marriage must always take place in the morning, but the betrothal is celebrated in the evening. Elaborate cards of invitation are issued, setting forth the parentage and titles of the parties to be betrothed, and all the friends and relations are prayed to be present, and assist at the ceremony. The palace is flung open and splendidly lighted and decorated with flowers, and the guests wear their richest dresses and orna-ments. When all are assembled, the marriage con-tract and papers conferring the dowry and making the marriage settlements are read aloud by the

An aunt and nephew, or an uncle and niece, cannot intermarry. An adopting parent cannot marry an adopted child.

But while the above restrictions on marriage are imposed, the King can, on due application, and as advised by the Court of Appeal, who make very careful inquiry into the circumstances, grant special permission for a marriage to take place between parties who otherwise could not legally intermarry. It is said, however, that such permission is granted to

notary, and formally signed by the notary and witnesses. Then comes the glad hours of congratulation. The bride and bridegroom are kissed by their friends, and all is gaiety and rejoicing. The marriage after this is more of a religious (and now civil) ceremony, and the bride and bridegroom, after a morning reception of friends, go off in their carriage to journey.'

only about one-third of those applying for it.

A marriage cannot take place without the consent of the father, or other legal guardian, when the man is below the age of twenty-five or the woman under twenty-one.

If such consent, however, is improperly withheld, the Court of Appeal, on application made, will grant permission for the marriage to proceed. Such applications are of very rare occurrence.

Before marriage, due intimation thereof must be given by a notice being affixed on the walls of the public office of the Commune or town. The notice is put up on two successive Sundays, and for seventeen days in all, it being stated whether it is the first or second time of

E

being posted. The marriage cannot take place till four days after the second Sunday of notice, and not after 180 days from said period; but in this last case a new notice can be put up.

The only legal form of marriage in Italy is the civil one. There are generally religious ceremonies as well, to satisfy the consciences of the contracting parties; and too frequently these are resorted to with disastrous consequences, especially to the ignorant woman, as such can take place either before or after the civil marriage. There exists at present a strong feeling that the religious ceremony should not be permitted till after the civil one, and legislation in this direction may take place in the near future.

The civil marriage proceeds before the

Syndic or his deputy, who must be furnished with the proofs of age and notice. He reads over to the parties the articles of the code relating to the duties of marriage, and asks them if they take each other for husband and wife respectively, and on an affirmative answer being given, he declares them duly married. There must be present at the marriage two witnesses for each of the contracting parties.

The Register of Marriages, which every Commune is obliged to keep, must then be signed by the parties before they leave the building. It is the duty of the Municipal or Communal authorities to see as to the registration of the marriage, and not that of the parties.

There is no obligation, on the part of either of the parties or their relatives to make any special monetary provision for themselves or their children in view of marriage, except in the case of an officer of the Army or Navy, who besides being obliged to obtain the special permission of the King to his marriage, must deposit approved securities with the Minister of War, yielding at least (1) in the case of a lieutenant, 2000 lire per annum; (2) 1600 lire in that of a captain; (3) 1200 lire in that of a major or colonel, and the same sum for all officers over forty, but officers with rank of general are exempt. This is paid to him during life, and after his death to his widow, and after her death the capital sum is paid to the children of the marriage, failing whom, it is returned to the heirs of the husband or wife who paid the money.

In view of marriage there may or may not be a contract. Should there be, the public register in which any mortgages, being the securities conveyed by the wife, are recorded, is specially marked, or if Rentes be the nature of the security, the certificate thereof is so marked; and these can on no ground be interfered with for other uses, except on application to the Court, which is only granted after a very searching examination as to the cause, and the then position of the parties. Except as regards such funds as the wife has so conveyed before marriage and brought under the contract, she is free to do with her property as she will, subject to the consent of her husband.

There is no action for breach of promise of marriage in Italy, except it be where there is a written promise, and then only for special damages, such as expenses which the injured party (man or woman) may have incurred in making provision by furnishings, etc., in view of marriage.

A child born out of wedlock is legitimated by the subsequent marriage of its parents.

British subjects can be married in Italy either by conforming to the marriage laws of the country, or by the Consul, in terms of the Foreign Marriages Act, 55 and 56 Vict. cap. 23, 1892.

NULLITY OF MARRIAGE.

An action for nullity of marriage lies (1) if the parties within the forbidden degrees marry; (2) if either of the parties was under the age at which it is necessary to have the consent of the father or other legal guardian; and (3) on the ground of incompetency.

SEPARATION.

There is no action for divorce in Italy.

The action of separation, however, can be brought on the following grounds: (1) Incompatibility of temper; (2) adultery by either spouse; but in the case of action against the husband, on this ground it must be proved that his mistress lived under the same roof as his wife, or that she is well known as his mistress in the neighbourhood; (3) cruelty, threats, and injuries, continuous and frequent.

In granting separation the Court can give orders as to the custody of the children of the marriage, giving or refusing the custody of one or more to either parent, or giving over the same to some neutral person.

CHAPTER V

SUCCESSION

In Italy there is no law of primogeniture, and an eldest son has no greater rights in his deceased father's property than the other children.

A father can on no ground whatever deprive a child of its interest in his estate at death, except it be that during life the child has received the equivalent of its legal share of the inheritance of its father.

On the death of an intestate male or female, survived by a spouse and children, the property is divided into as many shares as will represent the number of children and the spouse together. The latter then takes the interest of an equal share with the former, the children taking the other shares equally between them, and on the death of the spouse the share life-rented by him or her is divided equally among the children. Thus, if a spouse and four children survive an intestate, the estate is divided into five parts, of which the surviving spouse takes the life-rent of one-fifth, and the children at once take the other four-fifths equally among them, share and share alike; and on the death of the surviving spouse, the fifth of which he or she had the life-rent is divided equally among the children, share and share alike.

Should an intestate die leaving wife

and son, the widow receives the life-rent
of a third, and the son takes the other
two-thirds at once, and on the widow's
death he receives the third life-rented by
her.

The estate of an intestate survived by
father and mother, brothers and sisters,
but no widow or children, is divided into
three parts, of which the father or mother,
or the survivor, take one part, and the
brothers and sisters the remainder among
them. Should an intestate be survived
by no relatives up to and within the sixth
degree of relationship, his estate goes to
the State.

By will a father can leave only half of
his property to the prejudice of his wife
and children.

A surviving illegitimate child, when

legitimised by an Act of Court (see *infra*, p. 78), must succeed to the half of the share which he would have taken as a child born in wedlock.

CHAPTER VI

PARENT AND CHILD

In Italy a father is bound for the support of a child, who is also under his control till the age of twenty-one; and the father is liable for all debts for necessaries for his children up to that age, unless by public advertisement he intimates his declinature of such obligation. After the age of eighteen a child can apply for and obtain from the Court emancipation, so as to enable him to administer his separate estate or business. The father can name guardians to his children after his death, of whom no one can be a female, not even the mother.

Failing appointment of guardians by the father, the mother can appoint such, and failing appointment by her, the Court can appoint guardians.

An illegitimate child must be supported by the father and mother equally between them till it is twenty-one years of age.

An illegitimate child can be legitimised by an Act of Court confirmed by Royal decree, but in this case its rights of succession are limited (see *supra*, p. 76).

On no ground whatever can a parent disinherit a child.

ADOPTION.

In Italy, as in some other European countries, persons are permitted formally to adopt children on certain conditions.

The person adopting must have no legal children of his own, and the child must be, at least, eighteen years younger than the adopting parent, who must be fifty years old.

No person can have more than one adopted child, except all are adopted by the same deed. No one can be adopted by two persons, except by a husband and wife.

An illegitimate child cannot be adopted by either parent.

If a child be not major at the time of adoption its father must give his consent, and failing its father, the guardian.

The adopted child takes the name of its adopting parent, retaining, however, its own likewise.

Up to the age of twenty-one the adopting parent is liable for the child's support.

On the death of the adopting parent, the adopted child takes the same share of the parent's estate as a legal child does.

Before adoption, a proper contract between the adopter and the adopted, and its father or guardians, must be duly signed before the Court.

An adopted child can, with the permission of the King, succeed to the title of the adopting parent.

The adopted child is not barred from succession to its own father or mother, and does not lose its rights as a child of its own proper parents.

An adopting parent cannot inherit from his adopted child.

CHAPTER VII

THE NOBILITY

THERE is a class of Nobles in Italy, but they are not entitled to any special precedence in Court circles or public functions—precedence being given at such by virtue of office held. It is customary, however, to grant precedence to the nobility at minor functions.

Many of the nobles of the present day are the descendants of some ancient and distinguished families, such as the Massimo, who are said to be the descendants of Fabius Maximus the Cunctator; the Strozzi family of Florence, dating from

F

the 13th century; and the Sarego Alli-
ghieri family of Venice, descendants of
Dante, and dating from the 13th century
also.

The nobles are of five classes or ranks,
viz. :—

1. Princes.
2. Dukes.
3. Marquises,
4. Counts.
5. Barons.

The head of a noble house has alone
the right to be called by the title. There
is no second title attached to the family
except that of a Prince, whose sons are
called Don and his daughters Donna.

The sons and daughters of other noble
houses are known only by the name of

Signore or Signorina without any distinguishing mark of nobility.

The title of Duke or Marquis is often attached to, or connected with, a large estate in land. On the sale of such, it can be arranged, with the consent of the King, that the title connected with it be transferred as well—the former holder losing all his rights to it.

Additions are every now and then made to the members of the nobility. If a man has greatly distinguished himself in military affairs, or has given a handsome donation of say £4000 to an hospital, he will very probably secure for himself a patent of nobility which descends on his death to his eldest son.

As already indicated, there is no Chamber of hereditary legislators, and it may be, and is the case, that a Duke will be found in the House of Deputies, or Lower House of Parliament, while his untitled brother or neighbour is a member of the Senate, or Upper House.

The husband of a lady holding a family title takes the equivalent title—as, for example, a man marrying a Duchess takes the courtesy title of Duke.

DECORATIONS.

In Italy there are several Orders or decorations for merit.

The chief are as follows, viz.:—

(1) The Order of the Annunciata, which is the highest Order of merit, and stands distinct by itself. To it some Royal persons are presented, but of others only fifteen persons can hold it at one time.

The members of this Order are considered, rank, and are addressed as cousins of the King. They are called Cavalieri, are addressed as 'His Excellency,' and their wives as 'Donna.'

(2) The second order of merit is the very old one of 'St. Maurizio and Lazzaro,' which is given to persons considered sufficiently eminent in any way to receive it.

(3) The 'Order of Savoy' ranks next in degree, and is only bestowed on men distinguished in military affairs.

(4) The fourth Order is that of 'The Crown of Italy.' It was founded in 1861, and is bestowed on persons distinguished in matters military, science, and otherwise.

Each of the above Orders except the 'Annunciata' has five grades, and a holder can be promoted from one grade to another. The grades, beginning with the lowest, are as follows :—

(1) Cavaliere; (2) Ufficiale; (3) Commandetore; (4) Grand Ufficiale; (5) Grand Cordone.

An Order is conferred by the King on advice of one or more Ministers of State, backed by the Secretary of the Order. The presentees do not appear in the presence of the King to receive it except that of the Annunciata, but are simply furnished with the document of presentation. They provide themselves with the insignia of the Order, except when it is conferred *ex proprio motu* by the King, when he himself sends the insignia to the person so favoured.

No one can wear the badge of an Order of a foreign Court at public functions in

Great Britain or its dependencies who has not, before receiving it, obtained the permission of our Court to take it; and so in these places it is difficult for a subject of Great Britain to wear the badge of an Italian Order, as he, generally speaking, has it conferred upon him before he has an opportunity of obtaining permission of the Queen to take it.

CHAPTER VIII

RELIGION

By the constitution or 'Statuto-fonda-mentale' given by the King of Piedmont in 1848, which has since been extended by the Act of Union of the various provinces, the religion of the State is declared to be the Roman Catholic, but by the same statute it was enacted that all other forms of worship were to be tolerated.

At the present time (1896), the population of Italy is said to be about 31,250,000, of whom about 80,000 are computed to be Protestants, and 40,000 Jews. While the rest are supposed to be of the Roman

Catholic faith, at all events by profession;
but it is impossible to say how many can
really be counted among the 'faithful.'
There is very much Atheism and Scepti-
cism among the people.

All public offices are open to all persons
properly qualified, irrespective of religious
belief.

A traveller cannot fail to be struck, as
he goes through the country, with the
number of churches he sees, at the tops of
mountains, as well as on their sides and in
the villages at their base. He meets with
churches of all sizes and forms. While
attached to them, in some cases, are the
old monasteries or convents, which now
are often used as barracks, or for other
public purposes.

In Rome alone there are said to be

about 400 Roman Catholic churches, of which, however, many are now virtually closed.

That the priests exercise much quiet power is undoubted; but, it is said, not to the same extent that they do in Austria, France, or Ireland. At municipal elections they make their power felt, and often secure the return of their own nominee; but in elections for members of Parliament, as this body is alien to their views, their influence is felt only in the way of preventing persons from taking part in them. The Pope has in fact issued a Bulla or decree, called 'Non Expedit,' indicating this as the course of action.

There are many large private endowments, of various kinds, for religion, as well as those given by the State in former times, all of which are still administered by the State, and from which the bishops and other clergy receive their emoluments, or part thereof.

The bishops have an annual stipend of from 6000 lire up to 134,000 lire, but only one, he of Cefalu, has this large income, amounting to upwards of £5000.

The country priests, in addition to their monetary payments of from 300 lire to 20,000 lire—the average being about 1200 lire per annum—have a parsonage, and generally some land attached.

Before 1866 the monasteries and convents had large endowments; but the Government of the day abolished them all, and appropriated their revenues for public purposes,—providing suitably for life-interests,—and that for three reasons: (1)

because of the opposition of these institutions to the unity of Italy; (2) because of their number being greatly in excess of the needs of the community for them; and (3) because the country had need of the revenue.

Many of the orders of monks and nuns still exist, but it is as private bodies. They have no public or official recognition, and cannot as a body hold property. Such as they possess must be held by a private person, absolutely, in his own name.

Since 1871, in Rome, all Protestant communities can have their places of worship within the walls. Previously, they were not allowed to be within the gates— but had to worship outside. At the present day, any body of Christians or other sect can worship as and where they will, with this exception, that they must not, by preaching in the open air, impede the traffic.

There is, therefore, in Italy, full religious liberty and freedom of worship, unsurpassed, with few exceptions, by any other country.

Of Protestant Italian places of worship in Rome there are about twenty, while in the Kingdom there are about 450 in all.

The Protestants of Italy are to be found among six distinct sects, viz. :—

(1) 'The Waldenses,' who number about 60,000, and are chiefly to be found in the Waldensian valleys of Piedmont, where the large majority of whole parishes are among the adherents of this body. They have a training college of their own in

Florence. Their actual members[1] number about 20,000.

(2) 'The Chiesa Evangelica Italiana,' whose members are about 1500, and who have also a training college in Florence.

(3) 'The Wesleyan Methodists,' numbering in membership about 1400.

(4) 'The Episcopal Methodists,' who have a training college in Rome, and who have a membership of about 1100.

(5) 'The Baptists,' who have about 1000 members.

(6) 'The Chiesa Cattolica Italiana,' a sect founded in 1875, by Count Campello, formerly a priest in St. Peter's in Rome, but who left the Roman Catholic Church followed by a number of adherents to his views, and has founded this new body,

[1] By 'members' is meant persons in full communion.

which, however, does not make much progress. There are about 500 members connected with it.

There are various Evangelical agencies at work, chiefly supported by the British and Americans.

By about fifty Colporteurs there is a large distribution of the Scriptures and portions thereof in various parts of the Kingdom. In many places these are bought, read, and studied. In other places, when the priests discover that the people have been buying them, they insist upon the destruction of the copies, and sometimes there is a burning in public of those bought.

It cannot be said that there is a sensible increase of Protestants in the country during the course of the last few years. There has not lately been any great religious movement, and while there may be steady growth, it cannot be said that it is rapid. On the other hand, the Roman Catholic religion, it is said, is losing its hold upon the people, and many do not believe in its doctrines, while they do not adopt the views of other religious bodies.

It seems proper, in closing this part of the subject, to say something about the Pope.

The position of the Pope is clearly defined by the law of the Papal Guarantees passed on 13th May 1871.

By the first article thereof he is named 'Sovereign Pontiff.' He has, however, no territorial jurisdiction, but is supreme in the Vatican, although for crime proper against the State those dwelling under his roof and authority subject themselves on his call to the ordinary operation of the law of Italy, and practically the Vatican is under police supervision as regards crimes and offences.

The Pope never leaves the Vatican but if he did, he is entitled to all the honour due to a temporal sovereign. He sends Nunzi (legates) to many foreign Courts, and they in return send Ambassadors to represent them at the Vatican. Great Britain neither receives from, nor sends, an Ambassador to the Vatican. Her Majesty's Ambassador at Rome is in no way, as such, recognised by the Pope, and he cannot obtain for British subjects any special privileges from the Vatican. He is frequently applied to for such, and it is well it should be known that in this respect he is powerless to help British subjects.

Under the law of the Papal Guarantees, before referred to, the Pope is entitled to receive yearly from the State 3,225,000 lire, or about £129,000. He refuses, however, to take his allowance, although it is annually voted for him. And so, in the course of time (five years), it is again considered revenue of the country.

The Pope's income is to a large extent derived from Peter's Pence, collected and sent to him from all parts of the world. The amount is said to be from 6,000,000 to 7,000,000 lire a year, and not a small part comes from Ireland. He also has the interest of a large capital fund, invested chiefly outside the Kingdom, the amount of which, however, is unknown to the general public.

The Pope will not in any way recognise King Humbert as King of Italy, but only as King of Piedmont.

Except in the Sistine Chapel and in St. Peter's, the Pope takes no part in any religious service. English people resort to services at which he officiates in crowds. Admission is by ticket, obtained from his Major-domo, and some are sold to applicants by the hotel porters, who buy them from persons entitled to them who do not want to use them. The Pope appoints all the Bishops and high Church dignitaries in Italy, without reference to or with the approval or ratification of the King or the Government, except in the case of the Patriarch of Venice and the Bishop of Bari, and although the Roman Catholic religion is declared to be that of the State, the Bishops and other clergy do not now require to take any oath of allegiance to the King. For the enjoyment of ecclesiastical revenue by the beneficiaries, there must be the exequator, or authority, of the King; but in matters purely spiritual the State has given up all power and control.

CHAPTER IX

EDUCATION

In Italy, since 1871, elementary education has been compulsory in theory;
but as neglect to send their children to
school leads to no penal consequences
to the parents, it cannot be said that in
the rural districts all children attend
school, although in large towns, as a
rule, they do.

A school is required wherever there
are 500 inhabitants. The municipalities
are obliged to provide such, as well
as the salaries of the masters, from
their own revenues. And the Prefects

must ascertain that such provision is made.

It is a very rare case, and only in the southern Provinces, that children have no opportunity of going to school on account of distance.

Elementary education is free, and is given in large towns in two distinct classes of schools, viz.: (1) where books and material also are given, which are attended by the poorest children; and (2) where a small fee is charged, so as to keep the school more select.

In all elementary schools there are five classes or standards.

Any person having the appropriate diploma for the class of school he desires to establish, can set up a private school without permission of the Government.

All schools, public and private, are subject to Government inspection.

Besides the elementary schools, which are supported by the Communal fund, there are secondary and upper schools.

The secondary schools are supported by the funds of the Province, assisted by Government, and are divided into two classes, viz.: the technical and the classical.

The technical schools, again, have three sub-divisions, viz.: the Scuola, the Istituto, and the Scuola Professionale.

In the Scuola the curriculum is one of three years, and qualifies for shop and mercantile life.

In the Istituto the curriculum is one of three years, and qualifies as the Scuola does, but in a higher degree.

The classical side of the secondary school is divided into (1) the Gymnasium, and (2) the Liceo, and is attended both by male and female students, of whom the latter form about seven per cent.

The curriculum of the Gymnasium is one of five years, and qualifies for lower Government employment, and like occupations.

The curriculum of the Liceo is three years. It qualifies for higher Government employment, for teachers; and the leaving - certificate is necessary for entrance to the University and military academies.

When pupils leave the Liceo, they are generally from eighteen to twenty years of age.

The admission of female students to

the Liceo is a matter of recent years. The result has been most satisfactory; it acts as a stimulus to the male students, and stirs them up to greater exertions, so as not to be beaten by their fair competitors. Females attend the same classes at the same time as the males.

There are special upper schools for females, called Scuola Normale and Magistrale. These qualify for the teaching profession and for entrance to still higher female schools, besides which there are Scuole superiori femminili, of which there are only two—one in Rome and one in Florence.

There are also Scuole Professionali for young men and young women separate, qualifying for professional life.

The teachers of the elementary schools

are appointed by the Communes, and have salaries, in the rural districts, of from 800 lire, or £32, to 2000 lire, or £80, in the towns.

Teachers of the secondary and upper schools are appointed by the Government, those of the secondary schools having salaries of from 1200 to 4000 lire, and the others from 3000 to 5000 lire.

There are inspectors of schools, all appointed by the Government.

There are no School Boards, but the elementary schools are managed by the Consiglio Comunale, and the secondary schools by the Consiglio Provinciale, by means of a specially appointed officer, while the upper schools are managed by the Minister of Education.

There is a Council of Education, called

the Consiglio Superiore de la Pubblica
Istruzione, the members of which are
appointed by the Minister of Education.

Religion is taught in the schools only
when it is asked by the parents (one or
more, in theory), and that the Roman
Catholic only, by a specially appointed
teacher. Lately, the question has been
raised in Parliament whether the Protestants are not entitled to like privileges.

THE UNIVERSITIES.

There are in all seventeen State Universities (of which six are incomplete) and
four free Universities in Italy, besides
what is called the Istituto Superiore in
Florence for Philosophy and Medicine.

The following are the Royal Universities in Italy, viz. :—

Bologna.

Cagliari.*   Only three Faculties.   No Faculty of Philosophy.

Catania.

Genoa.

Macerata.*   Only one Faculty, viz. Law.

Messina.

Modena.*   No Faculty of Philosophy.

Naples.

Padua.

Palermo.

Pavia.

Parma.*   No Faculty of Philosophy.

Pisa.

Rome.

Sassari.*   Has only Faculties of Law and Medicine.

Siena.*   Has only Faculties of Law and Medicine.

Turin.

---

* Incomplete.

The following are the free Universities:—

CAMERINO. Has only Faculties of Law and Medicine.

FERRARA. Has only Faculties of Law and Medicine.

PERUGIA. Has only Faculties of Law and Medicine.

URBINO. Has only Faculties of Law and Mathematics.

Those designated incomplete are wanting in one or more Faculties.

The State Universities are dependent upon, and endowed by, the State; but the free Universities are not so, but depend upon and are supported by the Provinces and Communes, or by private benefactions.

There are no Universities proper in Venice, Milan, or Florence, although there are higher educational establishments.

The University having the largest attendance of students is that of Naples.

The oldest and best equipped of the Universities is that of Bologna, founded in the eleventh century.

All the Universities in all their Faculties are open both to male and female students, of whom the female students represent from about five to seven per cent.

As yet, however, although female students can study and take their degrees at the Universities of Italy, they do not as a rule make a practical use of their studies by practising the professions either of Law or of Medicine, in which they have taken a degree ; but there are in the larger towns now a few ladies practising Medicine. Many years ago the Professor of Mathematics in the University of Bologna was a lady.

A University with a complete staff has four Faculties, viz.: (1) Philosophy; (2) Law; (3) Medicine; (4) Mathematics.

THE PROFESSORS.

The teaching staff includes Professors Titolari (professors proper), Professors Incaricato (men who lecture during a vacancy), and Liberi Docenti, or lecturers.

The Liberi Docenti lecture within the walls of the University on the same subjects as, or on cognate subjects to, those of the Professors. The fees of the students are their only remuneration, but in the event of a vacancy in a Chair they have a very good chance of obtaining the appointment.

The Principal, or Rector, of the University is called Rettore Magnifico. He is appointed from among the Professors, who meet in council for this purpose once a year. The appointment is for one year, although generally the same man is re-appointed for two years more. This is the only occasion on which all the Professors meet together for business.

The affairs of the University are administered by the different Faculties, and by the Minister of Education.

There does exist, however, in the University a body known as the Consiglio Accademico, whose principal, if not sole, duty is to deal with the discipline of the University, before which unruly students are summoned, and if necessary receive punishment of rustication for a few months, or for a session, and in very bad cases the penalty is expulsion from all the Universities. This last is not of common occurrence, but occasionally the penalty is imposed.

The Faculty in which a new appointment to a Chair is to be made can, and often does, recommend a person to it, but the appointment is made by the Minister of Education, ratified by the King.

The politics of a candidate for the office of a Professor do not in any way enter into the question of his appointment, although he may be himself at the time of the vacancy a Member of the Senate or of the House of Deputies. The appointment is *ad vitam aut culpam*.

The salaries of the Professors vary from 5000 to 8000 lire, besides which they are entitled to the fees of the students, which on an average are 12 lire a course, and are paid to the Professors themselves.

The Professors of Law have the largest salaries and, at all events in Naples, the largest classes, where one Professor is said to have a class of 400 students.

The Universities of Italy do not confer degrees *honoris causa*.

The Professors on no occasion wear robes of office, and appear at public and State functions in evening dress.

There is only one session of the University, beginning in November and ending in July, with a vacation of three weeks at Christmas, and three weeks at Easter.

THE STUDENT.

The student enters the University upon the certificate of the Liceo, as the guarantee of his fitness, about the age of nineteen, and at once enrols in the Faculty in which he intends to graduate.

The curriculum for graduation in all the Faculties is four years, except that of Medicine, in which it is six.

In addition to his class fees already noted (p. 111), the student has to pay to general funds of the University, on matriculation for the first time, the sum of 60 lire, and, in addition, 160 lire annually. For his diploma on taking his degree he pays 50 lire.

There are, in each year in all the classes, two examinations in which the intending graduate must obtain 70 per cent. of the marks.

At the close of his curriculum he presents a Thesis to the Faculty on a subject chosen by himself.   If accepted as of sufficient merit for graduation, the author is summoned before the Faculty, and after being examined *pro forma* he is addressed by the Dean, and admitted to his degree.

There is no formal function for the conferring of degrees.

When a graduate obtains his degree he is generally twenty-three or twenty-four years of age.

The students and graduates do not wear caps or gowns.

There are in the Italian Universities no students' clubs, as in Germany, where beer is drunk *ad libitum* as a custom, but students' debating societies, chiefly political, exist.

Duels among the students as a recreation, as in Germany and Austria, are unknown. As a custom, there are no sports among the students.

There are borse (or bursaries) for students. These, however, are seldom given to the sons of peasants or the working classes, but to those of the better classes who are too poor to send their sons to the University, except with such help. They are, too, only given after examination to test merit and capacity.

There are no Colleges in the Italian Universities where the students reside, but they live in apartments, or with their parents or friends at home.

GENERAL REMARKS.

Generally, it may be said that, in the matter of education, Italy has made great progress during the past thirty years. In

1863 about 77 per cent. of the population could neither read nor write, and in some places the percentage rose to 85 and 90.[1] At the present time about 50 per cent. probably represents the number of those unable to read or write. There are about 2,500,000 children now under instruction in the public schools, and 500,000 in the private schools, which is more than double the number there was in 1862. Upwards of £2,500,000 sterling is annually spent by the State on education. In some places still, however, great ignorance prevails, and the most primitive methods of communicating ideas, and conducting business, as by notches on sticks, are resorted to, while the employment of the letter-writer is still a lucrative one.

[1] Probyn's *Italy*, p. 289.

CHAPTER X

THE LAND

THE land of Italy is held both by very large proprietors and smaller ones. The largest proprietor is the Duke of Ceri, whose rental is between five and six millions of lire. There is no law of entail in the country, and every owner of land can deal with it as he desires, by testament, donation, or sale. But while this is so, estates often remain for long in the same family, as a father can always leave to any of his children the half of his property in addition to a child's portion of the rest of his estate. (See p. 73.)

There is a very well kept Register of Land Rights, in which the description and extent of every estate in land is recorded, as well as its value.

Every deed of transfer, or mortgage, or deed constituting a burden on land, requires to be recorded in this register, and a recorded deed is preferred in competition to an unrecorded one.

The deeds of transfer, etc., are prepared by the notary, whose business it is to see them properly registered. The deeds require to be duly stamped.

The system of letting land varies in different parts of Italy.

In a great part of Piedmont, and in nearly all Central Italy as well as in the Venetian provinces, what is known as the Mezzadria System prevails.

Under this system the proprietor of the soil provides the land and the house, supplies the implements of husbandry as well as pays for half the seed and cattle, while the contadino (or peasant) supplies the labour, pays for half the seed and the cattle, and the profits are equally divided between them. This system is said to work very well, and both parties flourish under it.

Although the contract is only for one year, it exists in many cases during a long course of years, and even generations, with profit to all parties concerned.

As a rule, the contadino works the land with the help of members of his own family—including, it may be, his brothers and sisters, as well as his wife and children—only employing outside labour at seed-time, harvest, and vintage.

In Lombardy the land is let on lease in large quantities to an affittabile, for a sum fixed, who employs families of labourers to till the soil. The leases are generally for a period of about ten years, and the rents are of an amount which will yield a return of about three per cent. on the value of the land. The wages paid by the affittabile are miserably small—as sixty centimes, or about sixpence a day, is about the average amount, besides a house and garden-ground, the latter, however, being frequently of too limited extent even for the labourer's own use.

In parts of the Kingdom, chiefly in Piedmont, the land is owned and cultivated by small peasant proprietors.

In other parts the large owners till the ground by their own direct employees.

In the Campagna about Rome there is a class of men known as *Mercante di Campagna* who take on lease large tracts of land for the pasture of cattle and horses, and the growing of corn. These men generally live in Rome, and employ casual labour for their work.

The owner of the land, in all cases, builds the houses and offices, and keeps them, as well as the roads and fences, in proper repair when he lets the land.

In Italy there are no building leases, and if a person desires to build a house he must buy the ground on which it is to be erected.

For first-class mortgages on land the rate of interest is 4 to $4\frac{1}{2}$ per cent.

The interest given by banks on current accounts is between 3 and 4 per cent.

Succession duty is payable by the heirs or others succeeding to landed estates.

The game on the land belongs to the proprietor, and cannot without his permission be shot, or taken by any one else, provided he surrounds his property with boundary marks, and with posts at intervals bearing the word 'Bandita.'

To shoot game a licence costing ten lire is required.

Persons found shooting on land preserved as before indicated are deemed poachers, and are dealt with as such by law.

The fishing in rivers flowing to the sea is free to all in Italy. The fishing in small rivers, and in lakes within the grounds of a proprietor, is private, and can be treated as preserved if desired. They may be let to other parties.

The forests in Italy are the property of the proprietors on whose ground they are, but their rights in some localities, as to felling trees, are limited by the State.

There are inspectors of forests appointed by the Government, to see that the owners keep within their rights. There is a School of Forestry at Vallombrosa, near Florence, for the training of foresters.

CHAPTER XI

THE ARMY AND NAVY

THE peace strength of the Army of Italy is 280,000 men, 10,000 horses, and 900 guns.

The composition of the Army is as follows, viz. :—

2 Regiments of Grenadiers	}	There are 1360 of these Regiments, consisting of four Battalions and four Companies of each. The war strength of each Company is 250, and the peace about 85.
96 ,, Infantry		
12 ,, Bersagliere		
7 ,, Alpine Troops		
10 ,, Lancers	}	There are 400 in each Regiment, which consists of three Squadrons.
14 ,, Cavalry		
24 ,, Artillery	}	There are two divisions in each Regiment, of two Batteries each, and four guns in each.

2 Regiments of Light Artillery.

5   ,,   Foot Artillery.

4   ,,   Engineers.

12 Companies of Sanitary Corps

12   ,,   Commissariat.

12   ,,   Carabineers.

The war strength of the Army is 2,500,000 men.

It is divided as follows, viz. :—

Infantry, ...	2,170,000
Cavalry, ...	65,000
Artillery, ...	200,000
Engineers and Commissariat, .	45,000
Sanitary Corps, . . .	20,000

Besides which there are 51,000 horses, and 1700 guns.

Besides the above, in case of need, as a *dernier ressort*, the Communes among them must supply about a million men.

The annual levy for the army is about

80,000 men. From the age of twenty to forty all the men of a district not already enrolled in the army must present themselves for inspection and selection to the proper authorities in it, and a ballot for those to serve takes place, who, when found duly qualified, begin their service— all the others receiving in their own locality a drill of three weeks, so as to qualify them for emergencies.

For two years, in the infantry, and three in the cavalry, the service of those selected is regular, after which, during the next seven years, they are liable to be called on for duty.

A student at the University can have his regular service limited to one year if he pays a fine of 1000 lire.

During his time of regular service, a

soldier cannot marry, although he may at the time of entry on service be a married man.

The pay of a common soldier is only ten centimes a day (about a penny) besides his board and lodging, which includes wine and coffee, and his clothes.

In a regiment, serving in the ranks, will be found with the peasant soldier the sons of men of wealth and culture. They share the same barracks, and board, and are clothed in the same manner as their poorer brethren. It is said that the food is of good quality.

A man cannot elect to be a soldier for life, but only for a period not exceeding five years at a time. After twelve years' service, if he has obtained rank as a non-commissioned officer, he is generally preferred at the close of his service for some Government appointment, such as an usher in the Houses of Parliament, or as a caretaker of some of the public offices.

THE OFFICER.

There are three military schools in Italy where officers are trained for their profession—viz. at Modena for the infantry, where the curriculum is one of three years; at Pinerolo for the cavalry, where the curriculum is four years; and at Turin, which is principally for the engineers, but also for the artillery, where the curriculum is five years. The Turin institution is named an Academy. Before entering any of these seminaries a severe examination must be passed, that for Turin being the most difficult.

To pass out from these institutions another severe examination must be gone through, and then the cadet gets his commission, and joins his regiment at once. He cannot elect to join any particular regiment.

Italian officers must always appear in uniform, whether on duty or not, unless they are on long leave. The only exception to this rule is that of officers of the rank of general.

There is no Commander-in-Chief of the Army except during war. The Secretary of War discharges the duties of this office in times of peace.

The pay of officers is as follows:—

Sub-Lieutenant,	.	.	1,800 lire.
Lieutenant,	.	.	2,000 ,,
Captain,	.	.	3,200 ,,

Major, ...	4,400	lire.
Lieut.-Colonel, . . .	5,200	„
Colonel, ...	7,000	„
Major-General, . . .	9,000	„
Lieut.-General, . . .	12,000	„
General,[1]	15,000	„

The officers can retire on pension at the age of fifty-two, having served twenty-five years, and sooner if disabled in any way. The pension varies from half the pay to about eight-tenths thereof, according to the age at which he retires, and the period of ordinary service and amount of active service in war.

An officer's widow receives a pension equal to about two-thirds of her husband's pension, which, failing a widow, the children take among them till of age. If the widow marries again she loses the pen-

[1] He has 3000 lire for expenses.

sion, but the children take it till of age.

As previously stated, an officer desiring to marry must obtain the permission of the King, and must deposit certain securities with the Minister of War (see p. 68). This permission is not granted as a matter of course, but only after very careful inquiry as to the circumstances and character of the bride.

Duels, though not of common occurrence, occasionally take place among the officers. These must be of equal rank. When the occasion arises, their brother officers try to arrange the matter. If they fail, and the challenge is sent, as a matter of honour it must be accepted; but whether accepted or not, the challenged is subjected to discipline by his brother officers. The weapons used are generally swords. The result is seldom fatal; but if it is, the surviving combatant is subjected to punishment for a time.

The horses for the Army are generally bought in Tuscany or in Hungary for about 800 lire each. If an officer desires to purchase a horse from the Government dépôt he can do so at this price, and pay for it by instalments.

The rifle used in the Army is simply called fucile (rifle), modello 1891, rapidly loading, calibre m.m. 6·5.

There are two kinds of guns—heavy ones, calibre 9, and light ones, calibre 7·5. For the defence of the coast there are big guns as for the Navy, which is provided with the best and most powerful guns of 120 tons, made in England.

THE NAVY.

The Navy of Italy is a large one, and consists of 298 battle-ships, of which there are—

12 turreted ironclads,

4 ironclad frigates,

2 incrociatori, or large cruisers,

12 smaller ships, partly of iron;

while the rest are small cruisers and torpedo-boats.

There are 24,000 marines.

The annual levy for the Navy is about 3000 men, who are taken chiefly from the sea-coast districts. It is conducted very much as that for the Army, and the rules for service are very much the same.

The only training-school for naval officers is that at Leghorn.

The principal naval station in the Kingdom is Spezia, while Venice and Taranto are also regarded as important.

The pay of the officers is as follows:—

Midshipman,	. .	1,800 lire.
Sub-Lieutenant, .	.	2,200 ,,
Lieutenant, .	. .	3,200 ,,
Captain of Corvette,	.	4,400 ,,
,, Frigate,	.	5,200 ,,
,, Vessel,	.	7,000 ,,
Commander,	. .	9,000 ,,
Vice-Admiral,	. .	12,000 ,,
Admiral,	. . .	15,000 ,,

It is, however, only during war that the services of an Admiral of the Fleet are requisitioned, the Minister for the Navy directing the movements of the fleet during peace.

The pay of the ordinary sailor is 180 lire a year.

CHAPTER XII

COMMERCE, TRADE, ETC.

THE average of the exports of Italy during the last ten years has been about 1,000,000,000 lire, or about £40,000,000 a year; and consisted chiefly of raw silk, wine, oil, eggs, hemp, coral, sulphur, butter; fruit, consisting of lemons, oranges, grapes, apples, peaches, figs and pears, and cattle.

The average of imports over the same period was 1,200,000,000 lire, or £48,000,000; and consisted of corn, cotton, woven silk, coal, iron, hides, woollen goods, cloth, tea, coffee, sugar, tobacco, and rice.

The wine trade is very large. The production of wine in the Kingdom is said to be about the largest in the world, and is estimated at, on an average, about 400,000,000 litres annually.

There are comparatively few breweries in the Kingdom.

The chief articles manufactured in the country are paper, silk, straw hats, maccaroni, oil, artistic furniture, and iron goods.

There are marble quarries in various parts of the country, the chief being at Carrara. There are also granite quarries, the principal of which is at Baveno. There are likewise lead, sulphur, and tin mines in the Kingdom, and at Monte Amiata, near Siena, one of mercury. Aluminium deposit is also found in quantities; and salt is found in rock forma-tion, and is also recovered from the sea. Borax is also found.

Tobacco is a monopoly of the Government, of growth, manufacture, and sale; but permission is granted by the State in some districts to private persons to grow it, but only under strict inspection, and on the condition that they sell the whole amount grown to the Government, and that at a price fixed by it. Except in Sicily salt is a Government monopoly, both of manufacture and sale.

The Government grant licences for the sale of salt and tobacco, and in this way disabled servants of the Government or their widows, to whom a preference is given in the granting of licences, can make a small living.

The area of the Kingdom is about

70,816,142 acres, and is divided as follows, viz. :—

Mountains, ...	7,000,000 acres.
Uncultivated land, . .	6,000,000 ,,
Marshy land, . . .	2,500,000 ,,
Pasture, ...	3,500,000 ,,
Woods, ...	11,000,000 ,,
Cultivated land under plough,	25,000,000 ,,
Vines, ...	10,500,000 ,,
Olive trees, ...	3,500,000 ,,
Lemon and orange trees, .	1,500,000 ,,

The produce is as follows :—

Fodder, ...	14,000,000 tons.
Cocoons, ...	35,000 ,,
Tobacco, ...	4,500 ,,
Cheese, Butter, etc., . .	110,000 ,,
Wool, ...	10,000 ,,

The number of animals in the country is about—

Horses, ...	750,000
Mules, ...	300,000

Asses,	.	.	.	.	1,000,000
Oxen,	.	.	.	.	5,000,000
Sheep,	.	.	.	.	7,000,000
Goats,	.	.	.	.	2,000,000
Pigs,	.	.	.	.	2,000,000

The chief lines of Railway are now Government property. They were made at first by private enterprise, but in 1875 the Government bought up the lines of the Mediterranean, the Adriatic, and the Sicilian Companies, and then leased them out to new companies, who pay a nominal rent for them, while the Government guarantee from four to six per cent. to the shareholders.

The Postal Service is under Government, and the last return shows that 150,000,000 letters and 60,000,000 post-cards passed through the post in one year.

The Telegraph Service is a Government one; while that of the Telephone is a private enterprise.

Water is sometimes supplied by the Municipalities, and sometimes by private companies.

Gas and Electric Lighting and Power supply are the enterprise of private companies.

The Shipping of the Kingdom is a large undertaking, and includes about 6300 sailing vessels, with a gross tonnage of 580,000 tons; and 330 steamships, with a tonnage of 210,000. Genoa is the chief seaport of the Kingdom, and is making rapid strides in its trade, showing an annual increase of about nine per cent., while Marseilles shows an increase of only three.

CHAPTER XIII

THE RELIEF OF THE POOR

THERE is no regular State provision of any kind by direct taxation for the poor of Italy, and begging is forbidden, except to a few persons who, under the rule of the Pope, were allowed to ask for alms at the church doors, and who are still permitted to do so. These beggars may be recognised by a brass badge they wear on their arms. But although begging is forbidden by law, there being no penal consequences attached to its prosecution, it is carried on to a very large extent, as every visitor to Rome and other Italian cities knows.

The police occasionally apprehend persons found begging in the streets, and take them to the Police Office, where they are simply admonished by the superintendent, told not to do it again, and are dismissed. Thereafter they immediately return to their favourite occupation.

Persons who are not permanently resident in a place, when found begging, are sent on to their own home, or if foreigners, to the frontiers of the country. Many such persons are found in Rome.

Begging is found to be a very good trade by some. It is known of one beggar at least that he died owning two houses, and had 10,000 lire in the bank.

There are many foundations for the poor in the Kingdom, such as those for giving portions to girls when they marry, for helping young men in their studies, and for sick persons.

The hospitals for the sick and wounded are numerous, and are now very well administered under the direction either of the State, or the Provincial Council. There are asylums for orphans, the deaf and dumb, the blind and the lunatic, as well as reformatories for juvenile criminals, which are supported either by private benevolence or State endowment, but all are subject to inspection by the State.

There is no institution for idiots or imbeciles, of whom, however, there are, especially in the north of the Kingdom, a very large number. It is said that in the villages they are well treated and not molested. When it is found that an idiot

K

is unruly, confinement in a lunatic asylum is ordered.

In 1890 a statute was passed for the 'Opere Pie,' to regulate the administration of all the public charities of the Kingdom. Such are placed under the control of the Minister of the Interior (Home Secretary), and he can discharge any administrative body acting irregularly.

Irrespective of religious belief, the duly qualified sick or poor receive the aid they require from the proper institution. At least this is the law, but it sometimes happens that private benevolence must come to the aid of the suffering and destitute.

Should a foundation no longer serve its intended purpose, or be for the public good, the funds can be applied to a kindred object, or to some really useful public undertaking.

When the persons named for the purpose in the foundation of these institutions do not administer them, they are placed under the control of the Charity Commissioners, elected by the Communal Council, and they are all, as stated, supervised by the Minister of the Interior.

INDEX

Printed by T. and A. CONSTABLE, Printers to Her Majesty
at the Edinburgh University Press

www.ingramcontent.com/pod-product-compliance
Lightning Source LLC
Chambersburg PA
CBHW031117020726
47495CB00007B/2241